Zapped!
Danger in the Cell

Small Worlds Series

Book 1

By Jewel A. Daniel

and

Lynelle A. Martin

Illustrations by Ann-Cathrine Loo

St. Kitts born Jewel Daniel is a cell biologist, educator, and author who combines her love for science and books to teach kids about the exciting microscopic world of the cell. She also writes under the pen name Jewel Amethyst. Zapped is her first children's novel.

Lynelle Martin is a rising middle school student with an avid interest in science and adventure. Zapped is her debut novel.

CaribbeanReads Publishing, Washington DC, 20006
First Edition
© 2014 by CaribbeanReads Publishing
All rights reserved.
Printed in the USA
ISBN: 978-0-9899-3056-7
Cover and interior illustrations © 2014 by Ann-Catherine Loo
Cover Photo of Authors by D. Hughes
www.CaribbeanReads.com

This book is dedicated to the memory of a loving sister and wonderful aunt, Dale Antoinette Daniel (May 11th 1972 – May 1, 2014), whose unwavering support made this book possible and whose spirit lives on in our hearts.

TABLE OF CONTENTS

ACKNOWLEDGEMENT

This book is made possible through the hard work and dedication of many people who inspired, proofread, edited, or simply encouraged us in our quest to write and publish. Special thanks to the many families and children who read and gave us feedback while the manuscript was still in its infancy. These include the Macks, the Leaders, the Daniels, the Mitchells, the Archibalds, and the Ezins.

Special thanks to Carol Ottley-Mitchell who spent many hours editing, formatting, and making sure the book is in top shape for publishing. We also thank Alexa and Andrew Mitchell for their input and their frank opinions on the text and cover design.

We are grateful to our illustrator Ann-Cathrine Loo who spent countless hours revising each illustration to fit our numerous changes and learning about cell Biology to make sure the illustrations were technically correct.

Finally we thank our family and friends who supported us and encouraged us in the writing and the publishing process. Special thanks to Dale A. Daniel who suggested that I encourage Lynelle to write as a way of getting her to read more. We wish she was here to see the final product.

For everyone of you, we give a great big THANK YOU.

Chapter 1

The Field Trip

Lynelle looked around the huge lobby at the Museum of Natural History in awe. She darted from exhibit to exhibit, unable to contain her excitement. She hadn't been to the Museum before but she had been reading about it ever since her teacher, Mrs. Jones, announced they would be going there for the annual fifth grade field trip. This year, Ms. Simon's kindergarten class was accompanying them.

Lynelle joined the group of fifth-graders waiting anxiously for the teachers' instructions. She had to tiptoe to see her teacher over the shoulders of the taller students.

"I can't wait to see the bones from the giant dinosaur," Lynelle whispered to her best friend, Sonya. "I heard it's huge!"

Sonya put a finger to her lips and glanced down at Lynelle, "Shh! Mrs. Jones is talking."

"Today, we are going to be kindergarten buddies," Mrs. Jones announced. "Every fifth-grader must pair up with a kindergartener. You'll take your kindergarten buddy with you when you view the exhibits. You can explore anywhere you want to in the museum but you must be back in the cafeteria by lunchtime."

Lynelle ran her fingers through her dark brown hair, being careful not to mess up the cornrows that her mom braided every Sunday. She sighed.

"I don't want to babysit today," she said.

Mrs. Jones held up her hand.

"One more thing," she said. "Each of you must choose one exhibit and write a report on it."

The fifth-graders groaned.

"Seriously? Kindergarteners *and* a report," one student whispered. "I thought this was supposed to be a *fun* trip."

Nothing could ruin this day for Lynelle. She didn't mind having to write a report on an exhibit from this museum. She loved science and planned to be a scientist like her mother when she grew up.

"I think I'll do my report on fossils," said Lynelle. "There's a huge dinosaur fossil right in the middle of the museum."

"What's that?" Sonya pointed to what looked like a big ball with a piece cut out on one side. It had lots of odd shaped tubes running through it.

Lynelle read the label over the exhibit.

"It's a cell," she replied.

"Cells don't look like the globe. They're flat," Sonya argued. She shook her head and her ponytail of long black straight hair swung from side to side.

"That's because this is shown in 3-D, like in the movies we see at the IMAX Theater," replied Lynelle.

"So cool! You can see everything in it. It even has the parts labeled. I know what I'll do my report on. It'll be on the cell," Sonya said, walking around the exhibit and making notes in her pocket notebook.

Lynelle and Sonya were so busy observing the model of the cell they didn't notice that each of their classmates had chosen a kindergartener.

Mrs. Jones walked toward the girls. She held two children by the hand. She smiled.

"Well girls," she said. "There are only two kindergarteners left. Make your choice."

Lynelle turned around and groaned. The last two kindergarteners were her little sister, Giselle, and Sonya's little brother, Justin.

Giselle skipped over to Lynelle. The braids that hung from her two pony-tails bounced up and down. She placed her hand in Lynelle's and smiled at her big sister. Lynelle sighed.

"Come on Little Brat, let's go," she said. "I want to see the giant dinosaur."

"But I want to see the Hope Diamond," Sonya countered.

"Why don't we go see the dinosaur first, then we'll see the Hope Diamond."

"No. I want to see the Hope Diamond first."

The two friends argued back and forth.

Finally Sonya said, "Why don't all four of us vote on where we visit first?"

She turned to ask the kindergartners what they wanted to visit first but they were nowhere in sight.

Chapter 2

Lost Buddies

"Oh no, we've lost our kindergarten buddies!" Lynelle exclaimed.

The two girls hurried along the halls of the museum, frantically searching for the missing children. They passed an open doorway. A number of students from their school were inside.

"Maybe they're in here," Sonya suggested.

Lynelle and Sonya entered the small crowded room. A tall man in a white lab coat stood at the front of the room. He reminded Lynelle of the Jolly Green Giant pictured on the can of sweet peas her mom often served with dinner.

Giselle and Justin were standing in a line waiting to look into a microscope.

Lynelle and Sonya grasped their buddies' hands.

"You must not run off like that," Lynelle scolded her sister.

Just then the man wearing the white coat introduced himself.

"My name is Dr. Small, and I am one of the scientists working here at the Museum. Today I will tell you all about tiny things called cells."

"Cells?" a few students repeated.

"Yes, cells," Dr. Small continued. "All living things: plants, animals, human, are made up of really tiny things called cells. They are so small you can't see them without using a microscope. Microscopes make little things look really big. Cells are the building blocks of life. They take in food, they produce energy, and they let off waste. Most importantly, cells can make identical copies of themselves."

Dr. Small drew rapidly on the white board. First he drew a rectangle with a little tail hanging off. He filled the shape with small circles and then he added something that looked like a cloud.

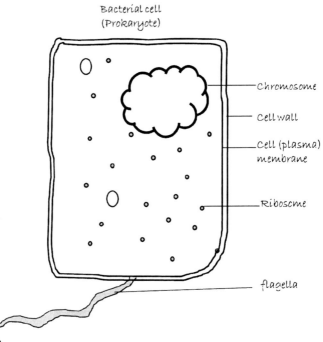

Bacterial cell
(Prokaryote)

Chromosome

Cell wall

Cell (plasma)
membrane

Ribosome

flagella

Next to the rectangle he drew a misshapen circle and filled it with many different shapes. Lynelle thought that it looked a lot like a flat version of the 3D model Lynelle and Sonya had just seen in the lobby.

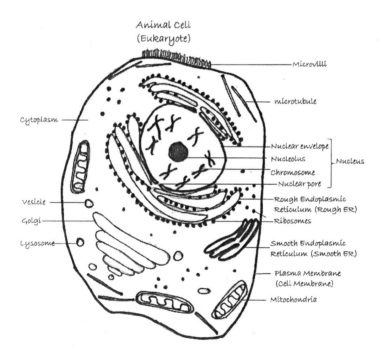

Animal Cell
(Eukaryote)

Microvilli

microtubule

Cytoplasm

Nuclear envelope
Nucleolus   Nucleus
Chromosome
Nuclear pore

Vesicle

Golgi

Lysosome

Rough Endoplasmic
Reticulum (Rough ER)

Ribosomes

Smooth Endoplasmic
Reticulum (Smooth ER)

Plasma Membrane
(Cell Membrane)

Mitochondria

He pointed to the rectangular cell.

"The simplest cells, like bacteria, are called prokaryotes. They don't have a nucleus," he said.

Then he pointed to the other diagram.

"The more complex cells-- for example, animal cells-- are called eukaryotes. They have a nucleus," he explained.

Sonya's brother, Justin, raised his hand, "What's a nu-cu-lus?"

Dr. Small chuckled, "Nu-cle-us. That's like the brain of the cell. It tells the cell what to do, what stuff to make and when to make a baby cell."

"Awesome!" Justin exclaimed. "They even have babies?"

"What separates the inside of the cell from the outside?" Dr. Small asked the older students.

They stared at Dr. Small blankly.

Sonya glanced at the notes she took when she saw the 3-D model in the lobby and raised her hand timidly.

"The cell membrane?" she suggested.

"Very good!" exclaimed Dr. Small. "The cell consists of many tiny parts called organelles. The cell membrane is like the skin that keeps all of the organelles inside the cell separated from the outside of the cell. Much like your skin keeps your organs in your body separated from the outside."

He pulled down a screen over the white board so that a new diagram covered the one he had drawn.

Dr. Small pointed to the diagram and said, "And this is what the cell membrane looks like when you make it really big with a super powerful microscope."

"Lollipops!" a kindergartener blurted out and the other students chuckled.

Lynelle looked carefully at the diagram. It really did look like two armies of lollipops with their sticks facing each other ready to fight. Scattered between them were an assortment of solid shapes.

"These things that look like lollipops are molecules of fat," Dr. Small explained. "The membrane is called the lipid *bi*-layer because there are two layers of fat molecules. The solid shapes are proteins that live in the membrane."

"Like turkey and ham in a sandwich?" A fifth-grader asked.

Another fifth-grader added, "With lettuce and tomatoes."

"You all are making me hungry," muttered a kindergartener just loudly enough to be heard.

The others laughed.

Dr. Small nodded and smiled.

"The round heads of the fat molecules love water so we say they are hydrophilic. The tails are hydrophobic. That's the opposite of hydrophilic. It means...?" Dr. Small paused expectantly.

"They hate water!" the children chorused.

"Great!" Dr. Small responded. "See how the tails are all hiding inside of the lipid bilayer? Do you know why the tails are hiding?"

A fifth-grader raised his hand.

"Because they don't want to take a bath?" he answered.

Everyone laughed again.

"You're right. Cells have water all around them, inside and outside. The water inside the cell is called the cytoplasm and the organelles, the parts that make up the cell, are all floating around in there. There is water on the outside of the cells too in a space called the extracellular space," Dr. Small explained.

He told them about the mitochondria of the cell that were like batteries because they produced energy. He then showed them a diagram of a nucleus that contained things that looked like X's.

"Who can tell me what these are?" He asked the students, pointing to the X's.

Lynelle waved her hand and bounced up and down. Dr. Small pointed to her.

"Those are chromosomes. They contain all your genes," Lynelle answered.

"You are absolutely right, young lady," Dr. Small responded. "Chromosomes are made up of DNA which has all the information needed to make a new cell just like the old one."

Then he told them about how proteins travelled in the cell through the maze of channels called the endoplasmic reticulum or ER for short.

"If you went into a cell, it would look like a giant maze. You could get lost in there," said the scientist.

Lynelle raised her hand and challenged him.

"Nobody can go into a cell. A cell is so tiny you can't see it without a microscope," she said.

Dr. Small gave a sly smile.

"What if I told you there is a machine that could shrink you down that small?"

"Yeah right! That only happens in science fiction movies," Lynelle countered.

The scientist just smiled.

When the presentation was over, Sonya and Lynelle stayed behind after the other students left to see other exhibits. They bombarded Dr. Small with questions.

"How do the cells make copies of themselves?" Lynelle asked.

"There's a stage in the life cycle of the cell where every organelle is copied," responded Dr. Small.

"What's an organelle again?" Sonya asked.

"It's the different parts inside the cell, silly, we saw them on the 3D model," Lynelle responded.

"That's right," agreed Dr. Small. "And that includes the chromosomes. So before the cell divides there are two copies of every chromosome. Then the chromosomes line up and separate so that each new cell gets a copy."

"Wow! That's amazing!" Sonya exclaimed. "I am definitely doing my report on the cell." Then she added. "Is there really a machine that can shrink people and zap them into cells?"

Dr. Small smiled that sly smile once more but he didn't answer Sonya's question. He handed the girls two glossy booklets.

"Kids, I really have to go," he said. "But this booklet will tell you much more about the cell and its organelles."

Dr. Small left the room. Sonya placed her copy of the booklet in her waterproof fanny pouch while Lynelle began reading hers right away.

Suddenly Sonya looked around and asked, "Where are Giselle and Justin?"

Lynelle looked around as well.

Their kindergarteners had disappeared once more.

***

"Ay Dios Mio!" Sonya exclaimed. "We've lost our buddies again."

Lynelle looked at her quizzically.

20

"That's what my aunt, Tati Maria says all the time," Sonya explained. "She's from Puerto Rico."

Lynelle shook her head.

"I knew they would just be trouble for us today," Lynelle grumbled.

The two girls left Dr. Small's room in search of their buddies. They stuck their heads in one room after another. Some doors were locked. Others were open and filled with interesting items. Lynelle was not happy that they were stuck looking for their siblings. She would much rather be exploring the museum, seeing the giant dinosaur skeleton, and taking notes for her report on fossils.

"Giselle! Justin!" Lynelle and Sonya called for the children in every room that they entered. Finally they found them in a small dark room.

When Sonya and Lynelle entered they saw Giselle and Justin standing near a long table on which sat a strange machine with many buttons and flashing colored lights. There was a microscope next to it. Under the microscope was a dish with a red liquid. Giselle was looking into the microscope.

"What are you doing in here?" Lynelle asked angrily. "I told you to stay with me!"

"Look at this, Lynelle," Giselle answered excitedly, not taking her eyes from the microscope. "These cells look just like Dr. Small's drawings."

Lynelle and Sonya joined Giselle at the microscope.

"This is so cool," said Justin, moving closer to the strange machine. He reached out to touch it, his index finger hovering over a big red button. "It looks like my video game! I wonder what this button does."

"Don't touch that!" Sonya warned, but it was too late.

Justin pressed the red button on the machine. There was vibrating sound as a long robotic arm unfolded from the machine and moved left and right as if it was searching for something. When it was pointing at Giselle, Lynelle, and Sonya a bright red light shone from the machine. Justin watched in horror as the three girls were shrunk into little tiny specks and disappeared.

Chapter 3

Where are we?

Sonya, Lynelle, and Giselle were spun around and around as if they were in a whirlpool. When they came to a stop they were no longer in the room with Justin and the strange machine. Instead they found themselves floating in a warm liquid that looked and smelled like the ocean.

"Where are we?" whispered Giselle.

Lynelle looked around. High walls surrounded them. The walls looked like enormous oranges dotted with tiny holes. Lynelle was still a little dizzy from the spinning and she wondered if her eyes were playing tricks on her.

"Do you think that machine really shrank us?" Sonya asked.

Lynelle shook her head in disbelief.

"You're really gullible," she said. "Dr. Small was joking. There is no machine that can shrink people."

"But how would you explain all this?" Sonya asked, sweeping her hand around her.

Before Lynelle could answer, a wave of salty liquid pushed against them and swept them toward one of the walls. They found themselves hurtling towards rows and rows of giant, tightly-packed balls.

"What's happening?" shrieked Giselle.

Lynelle grabbed her sister's hand.

"Don't let go," she shouted.

Another wave came towards them and this one slammed them into the wall. It turned out there was no wall at all. The girls fell directly on to the giant balls. They felt soft and spongy. Two of the balls parted and the wave pushed Giselle and Lynelle through the gap and into a thick, gooey, greasy fluid that reminded Lynelle of her grandmother's bacon grease when it cooled.

The sisters, still holding hands, steadied themselves and tried wading through the thick fluid.

"Where's Sonya?" Giselle asked.

Lynelle didn't answer. The wave that pushed her and Giselle into the fluid walls had separated them from Sonya. She wondered if she would ever see Sonya again. She held Giselle's hand even tighter.

She looked around her. With the huge balls above them and the gooey liquid at their feet, Lynelle had to consider the impossible.

'*Maybe Sonya was right. Maybe the machine did shrink us and zap us into a cell,*' she thought.

"I'm scared, Lynelle," Giselle whispered. "I don't know where I am."

"I don't know either, but I have the book that Dr. Small gave me." Lynelle dug into her pocket to retrieve the booklet. She tried opening it, but it was slimy and wet, and the pages were stuck together. She threw it into the liquid.

"It's no use," she said. "This is all your fault, Giselle."

"I'm sorry," Giselle apologized. "I promise I won't run off again." she said.

She plucked the booklet out of the goo, shook it, and tried cleaning it with her shirt before handing it back to Lynelle.

"Truce?" she said.

Lynelle smiled grudgingly, "Truce."

The sisters, held each other tightly for support as they waded through the gooey mess looking for Sonya. Above their heads and behind them, the large balls resembled tree tops in a rainforest. Long wavy ropes like vines hung down, making the path a treacherous obstacle course. The only sound they heard was the squeaking of their shoes as they sloshed and slid through the goo.

Lynelle looked up at the huge balls overhead. It seemed that each ball had two vines. In between the vines and the balls there were structures that looked like oddly shaped boulders. Some were large and round and were only between the vines. Others were long and twisted like the water slides at the amusement park. Those went all the way up and disappeared between the balls.

Suddenly they came to a clearing. All the vines seemed to end in the same place, like an open curtain, leaving them in a clear area of grease. Lynelle looked around hoping to find her friend. Perhaps Sonya had been swept into the fluid walls after all.

"Sonya!" she called.

There was no answer. The sisters looked ahead and saw that there was another forest of balls and vines.

"I don't want to go back in there," Giselle complained.

"Neither do I," Lynelle agreed. "But ..."

She was not able to finish her sentence before she felt herself slipping and sliding towards the row of vines across the clearing. She tried to stop, but she just couldn't control herself. She clung to her sister as she slipped through the grease, still calling Sonya's name.

They stumbled and tripped through the grease-filled second row of vines and came to the big balls once more. It felt like a magnetic force was pushing them through as the balls parted and they fell on their butts into an area of salty liquid.

"Finally! No icky sticky goo," said Giselle.

She tried to wipe off her jeans. Lynelle watched as Giselle emptied her pants pockets, removing a piece of candy, an eraser, a pencil, and a pair of scissors. They were all wet and covered with grease. She tried rinsing them in the water.

"What are you doing with scissors in your pockets?" Lynelle asked.

Giselle shrugged sheepishly.

"A good scout should always be prepared?" she suggested, recalling the Girl Scouts' motto. She placed the items back in the pocket of her jeans.

Lynelle shook her head and looked back at the giant balls through which they came. It looked so much like the diagram Dr. Small had shown them of the cell membrane with the lollipops lined up like armies waiting to fight and the membrane proteins like chutes stuck between them. Suddenly it all became clear to her.

"I know where we are," Lynelle said to Giselle. "The machine really shrank us. We're in the dish that was under the microscope. That greasy forest was the cell membrane. And those must be the organelles Dr. Small spoke about." She paused then announced, "We're inside a cell!"

The two girls examined the cell, checking out all of the giant organelles. Some were long and thin like logs, others were round, and still others had weird shapes like sausages or gigantic stacks of pancakes. Lynelle and Giselle were amazed. They had never experienced anything like this before. Then they heard Sonya's voice calling their names.

"Sonya!" Lynelle exclaimed. She had never been happier to see her friend. "What happened? Where were you?"

"The wave pushed me down a long chute," Sonya said. "Do you have any idea where we are?"

"I think you were right, Sonya," Lynelle admitted. "As crazy as it sounds, that machine must have shrunk us and landed us in the dish with the cells."

"So we're inside the cell?" Sonya asked.

"I think so," Lynelle said. "That chute you travelled on must have been a membrane protein!"

"Membrane protein?"

"Yeah, remember Dr. Small's diagrams? They are proteins that live in the cell membrane."

"Oh," she replied.

Sonya looked at the grease on the sisters' clothes and asked, "What happened to you guys?"

Giselle looked down at her jeans and said to Sonya glumly, "While you had fun on the slide, we walked across that yucky, gooey membrane thingy and now my favorite jeans are ruined."

The fifth-graders looked at the expression on Giselle's face and burst into laughter. But even as she laughed, Lynelle wondered how they would get out of the cell and what dangers awaited them in this strange world.

Chapter 4

No way out

Wading in the cell was like wading in the marsh behind Sonya's house. It even had the fishy smell of the marsh on a hot summer day.

"We're walking through Atlantis!" Sonya observed.

Lynelle agreed. Inside the cell was like an ancient underwater city, with buildings of all shapes and sizes contained by the giant walls of the cell membrane. Long tubes that looked like logs on a river slid through the liquid. Lynelle tried to remember what they were called. She struggled to separate the pages of Dr. Small's booklet.

"Try mine," Sonya said, removing her booklet from her waterproof pouch. The three girls huddled over it and began identifying the parts of the cell.

"Aha! Microtubules!" Lynelle exclaimed.

"Huh?" Sonya and Giselle said simultaneously. They both looked at Lynelle as if she had lost it.

"The logs on the water. They are called mi-cro-tub-ules."

"And there's the nucleus!" Sonya exclaimed pointing to a large sphere in the center of the cell. "It's just like the model we saw in the museum. I can't believe I'm actually walking in a cell!"

Around the nucleus, rows and rows of endless roadways twisted to form an enormous maze. Lynelle looked up from the booklet and pointed to the roadway.

"That must be the En-do-plas-mic Ret-i-cu-lum," Lynelle said slowly, trying to pronounce the word properly. "Dr. Small was right. The ER does look like a maze."

Giselle pointed to two balls, one sitting on top of the other. "Look," she said, "A gigantic hamburger!"

Lynelle laughed. She opened the pamphlet and found a picture of the hamburger-like structures.

"That's not a hamburger. That's a ribosome. It makes proteins and the ER folds the proteins."

"What's that little maze?" Sonya asked pointing at what looked like a much smaller version of the ER. "The roadways look like sausages."

Lynelle searched the labelled diagram of the cell on the booklet. "I think that's the Golgi. It says here that molecules travel through it on their way to exit the cell membrane."

The girls fell silent. It was exciting to be in the cell, but Lynelle suspected that they were all asking themselves the same question: how would they get out of the cell and go back to normal?

Giselle was the first to break the silence.

"How are we going to get back home?" she asked.

Sonya replied, "Maybe Justin will get help."

"Or maybe the shrinking is temporary and will just wear off," suggested Lynelle.

Sonya looked worried.

"I don't understand how this happened."

"Justin touched that funny looking machine and…," Giselle answered.

"I know, but why us? Why the cell?"

"Mommy always says everything happens for a reason," Lynelle responded. Then her face brightened. "I have an idea. Let's just go back out the way we got in; through the membrane."

The girls sloshed through the cytoplasm until they reached the cell membrane. They stared up at the high wall. They walked along the edge looking for an opening between the balls, but there was none.

They tried pushing against the membrane but couldn't even get the balls to move apart.

After walking for what felt like miles looking for an opening in the cell membrane, the girls sat on one of the floating logs.

Lynelle threw her hands in the air and exclaimed, "I don't understand how we got in so easily and now we can't get back out!"

"The wave," Giselle pointed out. "It pushed us in through the membrane."

"True," Lynelle agreed. "And there's no wave on the inside of the cell to push us back out."

"We're trapped in the cell!" Giselle cried.

Lynelle sighed. "We have to find a way out," she said. "We only have until lunchtime to see all the exhibits at the museum and I've got a report to do on fossils."

"And I've got a report to do on the cell," Sonya responded. Then she laughed, "I know why we're here!"

She jumped down from the log and began wading through the water again, this time away from the membrane.

"Where are you going?" Lynelle asked.

"To explore the cell," Sonya responded. "I have a report to write."

Chapter 5

A Powerful Experience

Lynelle and Giselle followed Sonya as she splashed through the cytoplasm.

"We should go to the nucleus first. I want to see the chromosomes," Lynelle suggested.

"Let's visit the ribosome. I want to see how cells make protein," Sonya countered.

Giselle chimed in, "I know what proteins are. My teacher says we need protein to grow and to build strong muscles. She says we get protein from meat and fish and even hamburger patties. That must be why the hamburgers are making it!"

The two older girls said in unison, "They're not hamburgers, they're ribosomes!"

"They look like hamburgers to me," Giselle mumbled.

Lynelle and Sonya ignored her. Instead they argued. They couldn't agree on what to see first.

"Hey, look, ships!" Giselle exclaimed, pointing to several long rectangular shaped objects floating in the cytoplasm. Before the older girls could stop her, Giselle darted towards one of them. Lynelle and Sonya splashed through the cytoplasm to stop her.

"Giselle, how many times do I have to tell you to stop running off like that?" Lynelle scolded.

Giselle gave her sister an apologetic look.

Lynelle opened Sonya's booklet and studied the cell diagrams until she found something that looked like the rectangular shaped objects in the cytoplasm of their cell.

"Mit-o-chon-dri-on," she said when she found it. "That isn't a ship, it's a mitochondrion."

"I remember Dr. Small mentioned that," Sonya said. "What did he say they did?"

"It says they're like batteries in the cell. They produce energy," Lynelle read.

Giselle grabbed her sister's arm and pulled her toward a mitochondrion.

"I want to see the energy!" she exclaimed.

The three girls entered the mitochondrion through its holey outer membrane, only to find another membrane inside. The inner membrane snaked through the mitochondrion like the banks of a winding river. There was even a stream of water flowing between the river banks. The three girls strolled along the banks of the stream listening to the sound of the water flowing.

"This is boring," Giselle complained. "I don't see any energy."

The two others chuckled.

"That's because you can't see energy. You can only feel it," Sonya explained. "The mitochondria use oxygen to burn food and release the energy. It is a process called respiration. There are tiny pumps on this membrane that produce energy. They are too small even for us to see."

"Oh yeah!" Lynelle exclaimed. "We learned about respiration in Science class last semester."

"That's still boring," complained Giselle.

As they walked closer to the winding river, Giselle pointed to a circular island in the middle of the water. It was shaped like the scrunchy that held Sonya's hair in the ponytail.

"What's that over there?" Giselle asked.

"O-M-G, it's a chromosome!" exclaimed Lynelle looking up from Sonya's booklet on to the giant structure. "I thought all the chromosomes were in the nucleus."

Giselle said impatiently, "Can we go now? I'm still bored."

The girls climbed out of the mitochondrion and waded toward the endoplasmic reticulum. They were so excited to get to the ER that they didn't realise that they were on a collision course with a ribosome until it bumped into them. A thick chain was sandwiched between the two balls of the ribosome like the meat patty between the hamburger buns.

"Yeah! Hamburger!" Giselle shouted. She started to climb up the larger ball. "And it's making a protein patty."

Sonya followed Giselle's lead and climbed up on to the top ball of the ribosome. Lynelle followed suit. From the top of the ribosome, they saw what looked like Lego blocks bringing chain-links and attaching them to the protein between the buns of the ribosome. When they looked down on the other side of the ribosome, they saw a thin ribbon. The ribosome moved along the ribbon like a train on its track.

Sonya quickly took out her booklet. The girls sat on the ribosome while Sonya read out loud how the ribosomes made protein. The girls discovered that the chain links were amino acids—molecules that built proteins—and the Lego blocks were helper molecules that brought the amino acids to the new proteins. The ribbon held the instructions that the ribosome read to make the protein.

Fascinated, they watched as the next amino acid was added to the protein. It was like looking at a construction site and seeing a wall being built, one block at a time. The girls felt the ribosome move along the ribbon and then stop with a jerk. It stopped long enough for the Lego to add another amino acid, and then the ribosome moved again another short distance.

"A Ferris wheel!" Sonya exclaimed.

"Huh?" Lynelle replied.

"It's like they're loading the passengers on a Ferris wheel before the ride starts. We move up a bit, people get in the bottom car, then we move up a bit more so people can get into the next empty car."

"Yeah," Lynelle agreed.

Giselle looked down. The protein chain was now so long that it hung out from between the ribosome buns.

"How can we eat protein if it's so much bigger than we are?" she asked her sister.

"It's only bigger than us because the machine made us so small," Lynelle answered. "The cells make protein, but all animals are made up of cells, so when we eat meat, we eat the cells and get the protein."

"Right," Giselle responded.

"This is awesome!" Sonya exclaimed leaning over to get a better look. "Look at that protein grow!"

"I can't see properly from here," Giselle complained. She got up and walked to the edge.

"Be careful," Lynelle warned.

The warning was barely out of Lynelle's mouth when the ribosome stopped with a jerk. Giselle screamed. Lynelle turned just in time to see her sister lose her balance and fall off the edge of the ribosome.

"Giselle!" shouted Lynelle, running to the edge.

Giselle grabbed on to the protein that was being made, her fingers barely grasping the chain. Her legs dangled above the dark sea of the cytoplasm that filled the cell. She looked down. Her fingers slipped down the chain.

"Help!" she cried.

"Hang on Giselle, I'm coming," Lynelle shouted, but the ribosome continued moving along the ribbon away from Giselle.

"What are we going to do?" Sonya asked.

Lynelle responded, "We have to save my sister."

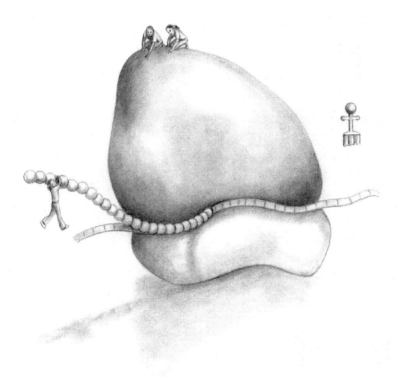

"On the count of three," Lynelle continued, "let's jump on to the protein and then crawl down towards her. Ready, one, two, three..."

The two girls held hands and jumped as far as they could on to the protein. They lay flat and crawled toward Giselle one amino acid at a time.

"Hang on sis!" Lynelle shouted.

Lynelle was out of breath when she finally reached near to Giselle.

"Grab my hand," she instructed.

Lynelle and Sonya helped Giselle on to the top of the protein chain. The girls straddled the chain and tried to catch their breath.

"That was close," said Sonya with a sigh.

Lynelle was about to respond when she felt a sudden jerk and the protein on which they sat began to free fall. Lynelle looked up and saw that it was no longer attached to the ribosome. The girls screamed and squeezed their eyes shut as they hurtled through the dark abyss, clinging on the protein.

Chapter 6

Dark Journey

There was a loud thud as their protein landed on the Endoplasmic Reticulum.

Lynelle opened her eyes and looked over at Sonya who was holding the protein so tightly that her knuckles were white.

"Look," Lynelle whispered.

Ahead of them was a tunnel that seemed to run through the ER. Lynelle remembered from the 3-D model of the cell in the museum lobby that the tunnel was called the lumen. The lumen curved and twisted and their protein was heading right for it, carrying the three frightened girls.

"You hear that?" Lynelle asked. Her voice shook.

The girls listened.

"I hear it," Giselle whispered. "Creaking. Like someone's opening and closing a garden gate."

"What do you think it is?" Sonya whispered.

"Look!" Lynelle said. Her finger shook as she pointed towards the protein chain. It was folding and twisting, and about to close around the girls like a giant python squeezing its prey.

"Move to the end or we'll be trapped!" Sonya yelled.

Linking arms, the girls ran as fast as they could toward the end of the chain that had not yet begun to fold.

As soon as they stopped, Giselle moaned, "It's so dark in here, I want to go home."

"Me too," Lynelle answered.

"But how? What if we never become big again?" Sonya cried. "What if we're stuck in here forever and ever? What if….?"

Giselle's scream cut off her words.

A monstrous protein loomed over the girls. Lynelle and Sonya looked at each other.

"Godzilla!" they screamed simultaneously, as the huge protein stamped a glob of oddly shaped molecules on to the end of the girls' protein, barely missing them. The molecules resembled a mountain of crumpled paper, but together they were heavy enough to weigh down the end of the protein chain. It tilted and the girls slid dangerously close to the edge.

"Back to the middle!" Lynelle instructed.

Lynelle, Sonya, and Giselle scrambled toward the folded center of the protein.

"Duck!" Sonya yelled as the Godzilla-like protein appeared in front of them. It stamped another chain of molecules on to the protein.

The girls screamed and scrambled back toward the end of the protein chain. The molecules caused the protein to fold even tighter into a ball. The girls were in danger of being trapped in the middle of a fold.

Sonya looked at the mountain of folded protein in front of them. It was no longer the loose chain that they initially rode.

"We have to climb to the top," Sonya suggested and she began climbing placing her hands and feet between the slippery crevices.

"Sonya, look out!" Giselle screamed as another chain of molecules attached to the protein

just above Sonya's head. Sonya ducked and then continued climbing.

Giselle hesitated. She looked up at the giant folded protein in front of her. Behind her, the molecules were being added and the chain was folding.

"I don't want to fall," she cried.

"Don't be scared Giselle," Lynelle said while comforting her sister. "Pretend you're on the rock wall in the school gym."

"But this is moving, and slippery."

"Don't worry. I'm right behind you. I won't let anything happen to you."

Giselle began climbing and Lynelle breathed a sigh of relief.

Suddenly their protein picked up speed and moved swiftly through the ER. The girls clung to the protein, ducking and dodging the molecules that were being added.

The protein on which they were riding came to a grinding halt. Lynelle looked around. The Godzilla protein was gone, so no more molecules were being added to their protein. The protein began to move again, this time slowly through the lumen of the ER.

The girls spotted a crevice in the protein that was shaped like a couch. Hand in hand they moved over to it and sat for a rest. They saw other proteins in the ER moving along in different directions.

"I wonder which way ours will go?" said Lynelle.

Sonya removed a small penlight from her waterproof pouch and shone it on the pamphlet. She read aloud that proteins were folded and modified in the ER with sugars, starches and fats. Some of the added molecules were signals that determined where the proteins would go. Some proteins went to the Golgi to be secreted outside the cell. Some went to the nucleus. Others went into lysosomes where they were digested by acids and special proteins called enzymes.

When Sonya looked up from the pamphlet, they were at the entrance of a dark small tunnel.

"Let's jump off," Sonya suggested.

Lynelle looked up at the tunnel looming ahead. Then she looked behind her at the wide lumen of the ER with its many branching pathways. She was afraid of entering the tunnel, but if they got off the protein now, they could be lost in that giant maze of the ER. Though she would never admit it, she was scared.

"I think we are safest on this protein. It's not being modified anymore," she said.

"But what if it is going to a lysosome?" Sonya asked.

"What's a ly-so-some?" Giselle asked. She hadn't really been paying attention when Sonya was reading from her booklet.

Sonya and Lynelle looked at each other. Neither of them wanted to scare Giselle but they didn't want to lie to her either.

Sonya said softly, "It's a bubble that has acids and proteins called enzymes that can digest things."

"Things? Like us? You mean it can eat us all up?" Giselle asked. Her eyes were wide with fright.

The two older girls nodded.

Giselle began to cry.

"I want to go home. I want my Mommy," she sobbed.

Lynelle comforted her sister. "Come on, don't cry Giselle. It'll be ok. We'll get you home to

Mommy, but right now we have to decide whether we'll jump off this protein or stay on."

Giselle pointed to the roof of the cave-like tunnel above them.

"It's too late. We're already in the tunnel," she sobbed.

Sonya and Lynelle looked around them and realized it was indeed too late to jump off of the protein. The tunnel barely had enough room for the protein to squeeze through. The protein creaked as it scraped along the sides of the tunnel, sounding like a roller-coaster going up the first incline. The three girls held each other tightly, closed their eyes, and held their breaths.

Lynelle's only thought was that if this protein ended up in a lysosome, they were doomed.

Chapter 7

Light at the End of the Tunnel

A faint light penetrated Lynelle's eyelids. She opened her eyes to find that the protein had burst through an opening in the dark tunnel and entered a lightsome cave. The floor of the cave was covered with clear water. Organelles of different shapes drifted around this compartment. There was a sphere in one corner and long coiled ropes in another. It was peaceful in this cave and the girls felt safe. Lynelle and Sonya looked at each other and smiled.

"We're in the nucleus," they said jumping up and down on their protein at the realization that they were safe for now.

They looked in the booklet. Lynelle pointed to a picture that showed a doubly thick membrane called the nuclear envelope connected to the ER by tunnels.

"Look," Sonya added. "It says here that only selected proteins bearing a special signal can enter the nucleus."

The girls looked at each other without saying a word. Lynelle said a silent prayer of thanks that they were on one of the special proteins and not on one that went into the venomous lysosome. Lynelle read a little more of the booklet then looked up and pointed to the sphere in the corner.

"There's the nucleolus," she said.

"What does it do?" asked Giselle.

"It helps to make ribosomes," Lynelle said.

"What are those ropes?" asked Giselle, pointing.

Lynelle looked up at the long coiled ropes.

"Those," she said, "are the chromosomes. They are made up of DNA and have all the information they need to form a new cell."

Sonya smiled.

"We're in the brain of the cell," she said.

The chromosomes were scattered all over the nucleus. Some of the chromosomes had two copies, a few had only one. As the girls' protein made its way through the nucleus, Lynelle saw one chromosome doing something different from the others.

"Look!" she pointed excitedly.

They watched in awe as the chromosome unravelled into two strands of DNA, separated like a zipper being opened. They saw the nucleic acids, the building blocks of DNA, attach to each strand of DNA. They formed two new zippers.

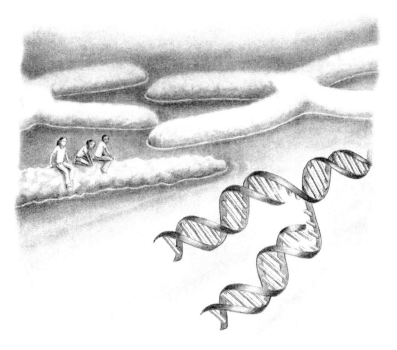

The girls' protein sailed right next to the new strand of DNA and the girls saw how it twisted like a spiral staircase. Then they saw proteins shaped like cylinders attach to the DNA.

The DNA spooled around them like yarn around a reel, forming two new chromosomes. The two identical chromosomes remained attached to each other by what looked like a bridge pulling the chromosomes together at the middle so that they formed an X.

"Wow!" Lynelle and Sonya exclaimed, their mouths opened wide in amazement.

"Wow!" Giselle repeated. "Twins!"

The protein that the girls rode sailed even closer to the newly duplicated chromosome. It navigated around the chromosome as if it had a mind of its own. Finally it docked onto the bridge.

Lynelle looked down at her pamphlet at a colorful labelled diagram of a chromosome. She looked up at the bridge on to which their protein had just docked.

"This bridge is the centromere of the chromosome," she whispered. "Come on. Let's explore the rest of it."

"Do we have to?" Sonya groaned. "This is so peaceful. After all the adventure in the ER, I'm exhausted. Let's take a little nap."

"Come on, Lazy Bones. You can nap later. Besides, don't you have a report to write?" Lynelle urged.

One by one the girls stepped off the protein and on to the centromere. They turned left and walked down one arm of the chromosome. It was like walking on an unpaved rocky road. They had to walk around the histones. These cylindrical proteins had wrapped the chromosomes when they were copying themselves earlier and now stood like boulders on the surface of the chromosome. The girls noticed that *all* of the chromosomes now had two copies, just like the chromosome they were on.

As the girls explored the chromosome, they noticed that it was getting fatter, thicker, and shorter. Then they heard a loud explosion.

"Wowza!" Lynelle exclaimed. The sound came from the nucleolus, the small sphere in the center of the nucleus. The girls looked over just in time to see the nucleolus disappear before their eyes.

Lynelle turned to Sonya.

"What's happening?" she shouted over the noise of the explosion.

"I don't know," Sonya replied. She removed her book from her pouch and began turning the pages frantically.

"Ow!" Giselle exclaimed as debris rained down on the girls.

They looked around them in time to see the nuclear envelope, the membrane around the nucleus, breaking down to pieces.

Sonya nudged Lynelle and pointed to a picture in the book. The two girls looked at each other and exclaimed at the same time, "Mitosis!"

Chapter 8

Separated

Giselle looked at the two fifth graders and asked, "What's mitosis?"

Lynelle grabbed the booklet from Sonya and scanned the page. She closed the booklet and looked around before answering Giselle's question. Not only had the chromosomes become short and fat, but the nucleolus and the nuclear envelope surrounding the nucleus had disappeared leaving the girls in a large open space where they could see all the cell organelles and the cell membrane in the distance.

"Mitosis is cell division," Lynelle replied to her sister. "That means the cell is going to split apart and form two new cells. We just passed the first stage called prophase. That's why the chromosomes got fatter and the nucleolus and nuclear membrane disappeared."

Lynelle showed Giselle and Sonya a series of glossy drawings in the booklet. The first picture showed the chromosomes as X's scattered all over the nucleus and no nuclear membrane. Under it was the word 'Prophase'.

The next drawing, labelled 'Metaphase', had the X's lined up in the center of the cell. The third drawing showed the X's had broken apart so they looked like V's and were far from each other. Underneath it was the caption, 'Anaphase'. The last picture showed two normal cells and was labelled Telophase.

Lynelle read the paragraph under the pictures, "In Telophase, which is the end of mitosis,

Prophase	Chromosomes appear condensed and are scattered around the nucleus. The nucleolus disappears and the nuclear envelope breaks down.
Metaphase	Chromosomes line up along the equator or center of the cell. Microtubules attach each chromatid of chromosome to opposite poles
Anaphase	The chromatids of each chromosome separate and move to opposite poles
Telophase	Chromosomes are no longer condensed. The nuclear envelope and the nucleolus reform. Chromosomes scatter around the new nucleus.
Cytokinesis	Splitting of the cytoplasm. The cell membrane splits and two new cells are formed. The new cells can now move away from each other.

the nuclear envelope will reform around the two sets of chromosomes and so there are two new cells."

"What's a nuclear envelope?" Giselle asked. Lynelle could tell from the way her little sister frowned that she was having great difficulty following all of this information.

"It's that wall around the nucleus that just broke apart and dropped all that debris on us," Lynelle answered.

"Oh," Giselle said.

"It will be rebuilt around each set of chromosomes. Then the cell membrane and the cytoplasm will split in a process called 'cytokinesis'." She looked up at her sister and her best friend and said in a serious tone, "This means we have to stay together at all times, or we can end up in two different cells."

Giselle placed her hand in her sister's palm. There was no way she was going to be separated from her big sister.

Several of the chromosomes began moving toward the center of the cell, lining up like players on a football field. The three girls stood still on their chromosome and observed the activity.

They saw logs float toward the centromere, the bridge that connected the chromosomes to each other. The logs stuck to the bridge and seemed to stretch all the way to the end of the cell. To Lynelle, it resembled a globe with the chromosomes at the equator and the lines of longitude going toward the north and south poles.

"Look, all the X's are lining up!" Giselle shouted excitedly pointing at the chromosomes moving quickly to the center of the cell.

"We're going into metaphase," Sonya observed.

The girls heard a thud, and their chromosome shook as if an earthquake had occurred. A log had just attached to the centromere of the chromosome they were on.

"What's that?" Giselle asked, pointing to the log.

"That's a microtubule," Lynelle answered. Their chromosome was the only one not yet lined up in the center of the cell.

"See how all the other chromosomes line up as soon as the logs attach?" Lynelle continued.

"We'll be moving to the center soon. Hang on tight!"

Even though Lynelle was expecting the chromosome to move, she was not prepared for the speed with which it was whipped to the center of the cell. She lost her balance and tumbled off of her spot.

She screamed. Her hands and feet flailed as she tumbled past the centromere. She grabbed the first thing she saw. It was a Histone, sticking out like a barrel on the other chromosome. Shaken, Lynelle pulled herself up on to the chromosome. She lay there trying to catch her breath.

She looked around for her sister and friend. They were nowhere near her.

"Giselle? Sonya?" she called.

She heard their shouts. They sounded far away. Then she saw them on the other the chromosome holding on tightly to a boulder-shaped Histone.

Lynelle tried not to panic. She had fallen on to the opposite chromosome and unless she did something about it, she would end up in a different cell from Giselle and Sonya.

"I've got to get back," she mumbled.

She scrambled to her feet and ran along the chromosome arm toward the centromere bridge. She had to cross the centromere and get over to the chromosome that Sonya and Giselle were on before the chromosomes separated during anaphase.

Getting to the bridge was like going through an obstacle course as she stumbled over histones protruding from the surface of the chromosome, but she did it and reached the centromere. She could see Giselle and Sonya on the other side.

"Hang on I'm coming," she shouted to them.

As she placed her foot on the bridge between the centromeres the ground gave way beneath her. She grasped a protein on the chromosome. When Lynelle looked up, the bridge was gone and the chromosomes were drifting apart. She could see the panicked look on her sister's face.

"Jump!" Sonya yelled to Lynelle.

Lynelle's chromosome was moving farther away from the one Sonya and Giselle were standing on. The gulf was widening. The jump seemed impossible.

"I can't," she shouted.

She stood helplessly as her chromosome drifted away from Sonya and Giselle. She looked around for something to use when she saw Giselle lean over the edge of the chromosome.

"No Giselle!" she shouted to her sister. "Stop her, Sonya."

"We have to do something!" Giselle shouted to Lynelle. Laying flat on her belly, Giselle stretched over the edge of the chromosome and tried to grab on to a microtubule just out of her reach. "Hold my feet, Sonya."

"She's too far away," Sonya responded.

"It's the only way," Giselle replied. "I have to help my sister."

"But you could fall," Sonya pleaded.

Giselle looked back at Sonya.

"Please, we must do something. Help me."

Sonya balanced herself between two histones and grabbed Giselle's legs.

Reaching as far out as she could, Giselle grabbed the end of a microtubule and pulled it toward her. She and Sonya anchored the microtubule between two rock-like histones on the chromosomes and guided the other end toward Lynelle.

"Grab this!" she shouted to Lynelle.

Lynelle was surprised at her little sister's bravery and her strength.

"Are you sure this is a good idea?" she asked.

"Just hold it!" Sonya shouted back. With the chromosome moving farther apart there was no time for discussion.

Lynelle grabbed the microtubule and Sonya and Giselle pulled it toward them. When Lynelle was close enough, her sister and friend held her hand and helped her on to their chromosome. As soon as she had planted her feet on the chromosome, it picked up speed and moved rapidly to the edge of the cell.

The girls lay on the chromosome. They were exhausted. The microtubules that once held the chromosomes together broke apart into little pieces. The nuclear membrane reformed around them as the cells entered telophase.

Finally, the cell membrane split as the final stages of mitosis took place. Lynelle felt the cell they were in moving and figured it must be the end of mitosis when the two cells finally unstuck and moved away from each other.

Lynelle smiled at her sister.

"Thank you, Little Brat," Lynelle said. "You saved my life."

Giselle smiled, "I couldn't lose my favorite sister."

"I'm your *only* sister," Lynelle laughed.

All three girls laughed and hugged.

"Now we've got to get out of this cell. I think that may be our only hope of getting out of this situation," Sonya said.

"So what's the plan?" Giselle asked.

Sonya and Lynelle looked at each other and shrugged. They had no idea.

Chapter 9

Escape

After a long discussion, Lynelle and Sonya agreed on a plan. They noticed that molecules came in and out of the nuclear pore, the tunnel through which they had entered the nucleus. Their plan was to hitch a ride on a molecule exiting the nucleus. Once they entered the ER, they would jump on a protein going to the Golgi.

They knew from reading the booklet that Dr. Small had given them, that the proteins in the Golgi were packaged in bubbles called vesicles and sorted like mail at the post office. Some proteins in the vesicles went to the cell membrane and were pushed outside of the cell. If they got on one of those they would be home free.

A few minutes later they were exiting the nucleus through the nuclear pore and entering the ER riding on a round protein. As they rode through the ER, they saw molecules travelling in different directions. A long protein came close to them.

"Ok," said Sonya. "When I give the signal, we jump on to that protein."

"Why that protein?" Lynelle asked.

Sonya responded confidently, "It looks just like the chute that I came through when I entered the cell. I think that's a membrane protein. It has to be going to the cell membrane."

The girls waited for the protein to pass near to them.

"Jump!" Sonya instructed and the three girls jumped onto the long coiled protein.

From there it was smooth sailing to the Golgi. The girls watched as proteins, fats and starches lined up next to the membrane of the Golgi. The membrane formed little bubbles around the molecules. The bubbles broke off from the Golgi, sending them into the cytoplasm of the cell. They noticed that some went to lysosomes. While they waited in line to approach the Golgi, Sonya and Lynelle read the booklet.

"I'm bored," Giselle complained.

"Count sheep," Lynelle said dismissively.

"There are no sheep here."

"Use your imagination."

Giselle sat and counted the different molecules getting wrapped in vesicles.

She tugged at Lynelle's sleeve.

"Lynelle," she said. "I think we're going into the bad bubble."

Lynelle turned to Giselle. "Why?"

"I see a pattern. All the proteins going to the bad bubbles have the same number and shape of molecules on their tails. It's different from the ones going into the good bubbles."

Giselle pointed to the marker on the tail of their protein.

"Ours is just like the ones going into the bad vesicle," she said.

"Sonya we have got to get off, I think our protein is headed for a lysosome."

"That can't be," Sonya argued, not wanting to admit that she had been wrong.

"Look at the pattern Giselle found, Sonya," Lynelle said, describing Giselle's observation.

"We've got to get off now!"

The girls jumped on to another protein.

"I think we're safe now," Lynelle said.

There was no response. When she looked around, Sonya was nowhere to be found.

"Where's Sonya?" Lynelle asked her sister.

Giselle pointed to the protein they had been traveling on earlier. It was about to enter a lysosome and Sonya was still on it.

"Oh no! We've got to help her."

Lynelle and Giselle jumped from protein to protein, until they reached near to Sonya.

"Jump!" Lynelle instructed.

"I can't. I'm trapped," Sonya shouted back.

When they looked they saw that Sonya's long ponytail was tangled in a fold of the protein.

"Wait here, Giselle, I'm going to help her."

"But she's already entering the bad vesicle," Giselle wailed.

Lynelle didn't listen. She stepped on to the protein next to Sonya and tried untangling her hair. It was firmly stuck and the lysosome was already forming around the protein they were on. There was a noxious smell like rotting eggs coming from within the lysosome. Lynelle heard a gurgling sound that reminded her of the volcano they visited on their trip to Hawaii last summer. She saw the fear in Sonya's eyes.

"Pull, I'll pull with you," Lynelle instructed Sonya, her hands trembling. They had to hurry before they were digested with the protein.

Lynelle tugged and tugged but it was no use. The membrane of the lysosome was now just inches away from her and Sonya when she heard Giselle say, "Here catch!"

Lynelle looked up in time to see a pair of scissors floating through the air. She caught it with one hand.

"Good catch," Giselle shouted.

"What are you going to do with that?" Sonya asked.

"Cut your hair," Lynelle replied.

"Not my..."

In a second she had cut the end of Sonya's pony tail.

"...hair," Sonya finished forlornly.

There was no time to waste. The lysosome was almost at their feet. The girls jumped off the protein and joined Giselle. They turned just in time to see the lysosome swallow the protein whole.

Sonya breathed a sigh of relief.

"Whew! That was close," Sonya said running her hands through the uneven ends of her hair. She turned to her friends and smiled, "You saved my life. Where did you get those scissors?"

Giselle responded with a smile, "A good scout is always prepared."

"Thank you guys. You are the best friends I can ever have," Sonya said embracing the sisters.

Lynelle laughed, "Just wait 'til you look in the mirror."

The membrane of the Golgi folded around the protein they were on, forming a bubble. The bubble broke off from the membrane leaving them enclosed in a new vesicle. Soon they were floating in the cytoplasm like a shuttle in space.

A few minutes later, the girls felt a bump as their vesicle docked on the cell membrane. The membrane of the vesicle fused with the cell membrane. Like a shuttle being opened, the membrane opened and the girls stepped out into the extracellular space. They had escaped the cell, but they had no idea how they would get back to their regular size and get back home.

Chapter 10

Tall Tales

When the girls disappeared from the lab Justin stared at the dish under the microscope for a long time trying to figure out what had happened.

"Sonya," he called.

There was no answer.

"Giselle, Lynelle, Sonya, where are you?" he called again.

He decided that he had to get help. He ran out of the room to find his teacher, Ms. Simon, but he had the bad luck of bumping into Mrs. Jones, the fifth grade teacher, instead.

"Where's your fifth grade buddy?" Mrs. Jones demanded.

Justin began to shake and stutter. "I...I...c... can't find her."

"Well let's go find her then," Mrs. Jones suggested taking his hand firmly in hers.

"They got zapped by a machine and were shrunk. Now they've disappeared."

"Wait who?"

"Giselle, Lynelle, and Sonya."

"Are you telling tall tales, young man?"

"I swear, I'm telling the truth."

"You know I don't tolerate fibs," Mrs. Jones scolded.

"But..."

"No buts," Mrs. Jones shook her head in disbelief.

"You've got to believe me, Mrs. Jones," he pleaded. He was close to tears.

"Well then, why don't you show me this mysterious machine?"

Justin led Mrs. Jones to the small room where he'd last seen his sister and her friends. Mrs. Jones turned the knob on the door. It was locked. The only way to open it was by punching numbers in a key pad on the door.

She looked at Justin sternly. "Are you certain this is the room?"

Justin nodded and kept his head down.

"Let me see if I've got this right. Your fifth grade buddies and you entered this locked room, they got shrunk by a magical machine, and you escaped through this same locked door?"

Justin hung his head.

"And you expect me to believe that?"

"Please Mrs. Jones, I'm telling the truth."

"Come with me, young man. You're going to stay with me until you learn how to tell fantasy from reality."

Justin had no idea what to do. Just then he remembered Dr. Small, the scientist, talking about a machine that could shrink people. He knew that Dr. Small would believe him, but he had no idea where to find him.

Mrs. Jones took Justin around to some of the exhibits with her. Then she took him down to the cafeteria with her and gave him a sandwich for lunch while she waited for the other students to return.

His teacher, Miss Simon, joined Mrs. Jones at the table. "What's he in for?" she asked smiling.

Mrs. Jones shook her head.

"He got separated from his buddy and now he's telling some tall tale about her shrinking."

Miss Simon chuckled. "Yes, Justin does have an active imagination."

Justin thought quickly. He had to escape. He had to find Dr. Small. He had to rescue his sister and best friends.

He got up from the table and began shifting from one foot to the other.

"Mrs. Jones, can I go to the bathroom."

Mrs. Jones looked up from her sandwich and saw him dancing about like he was about to have an accident.

"Ok you can go," she said. "But make sure you're back here in five minutes."

"I don't have a watch, Mrs. Jones, and we haven't learned time as yet."

"Count slowly to three hundred. That would be five minutes."

"Yes Ma'am," Justin answered and headed in the direction of the bathrooms. As soon as Mrs. Jones turned back to her sandwich, he ran out of the cafeteria.

He went to the lecture room where he'd seen Dr. Small before, but it was closed. He stood outside trying to figure out what to do next.

"Fifty-nine," he counted.

He was about to turn back to the cafeteria when he saw Dr. Small pass by the end of the hallway.

Justin ran toward the scientist.

"Dr. Small," Justin called.

The scientist kept walking.

Justin sped up until he caught up with him.

"Dr. Small I ..."

Before Justin could finish the sentence Dr. Small said, "Sorry buddy, I'm about to leave for the day."

"Dr. Small I really need your help," Justin persisted.

"I'm in a hurry," Dr. Small responded and kept walking.

He was about to exit the building when Justin blurted out, "Your machine shrunk my sister!"

Dr. Small stopped midstride. He turned and returned to where Justin stood. He stooped down until he was face to face with the young boy.

"Pardon me, young fellow?" he said.

"My sister and her friends, Lynelle and Giselle, were in the room with the machine and I accidentally touched a button and the machine shrunk them. Now they've disappeared in the dish under the microscope."

Dr. Small was silent.

"How long ago was this?" he said finally.

Justin shrugged, "Before lunch?"

"Let's go," Dr. Small said, taking Justin's hand. He had a worried expression on his face that made Justin nervous. "We don't have much time to make them big again."

Chapter 11

All's Well that Ends Well

Justin and Dr. Small arrived at the room in which Justin had last seen his sister. Dr. Small pressed a series of numbers on the keypad and the door opened.

The room was quiet, and dark except for an eerie green glow emanating from the strange machine. Justin shivered.

"They were standing right here, I pressed this button..." Justin ran to the machine to show him the button.

"Whoa there, young man! We don't touch anything in this room," Dr. Small said.

Justin hid his hands in his pockets and mumbled, "Sorry Sir."

104

Dr. Small moved around the room turning on machines.

"Are you sure they went into that plate?" He asked pointing to the plate of cells sitting under the microscope.

"I...I...thinks so, Sir. They were standing right over there."

Dr. Small nodded. He turned on a computer that was attached to a camera on the microscope. He tinkered with the microscope and the cells came into view on the computer screen. He shook his head and clicked his tongue.

"This magnification isn't high enough," he said.

"Sir, you've done this before, right?"

Dr. Small shook his head.

"Only on mice," he replied.

Dr. Small rose and removed the plate from the microscope. He placed it on a stand and focused a light on the dish. He handed Justin a pair of darkened goggles.

"You'll need these."

He pressed a button and a bright light flashed on to the plate. Suddenly there was a low rumbling and Giselle, followed by Lynelle and Sonya tumbled off the stand and on to the floor.

The girls got up and looked around dazed by the bright light. Sonya was the first to see her brother.

"Justin!" she squealed and ran to hug him.

"Ewww!" he exclaimed. "You're wet!"

"We're big again!" Lynelle and Giselle jumped up and down hugging each other. Then they hugged Justin and Sonya.

"I'm sorry I touched the button," Justin said.

Lynelle and Sonya smiled at each other and then back at Justin. Sonya said to him, "It's okay, Justin. It was the most fun I've ever had."

Talking at the same time, the three girls told Justin about the exciting adventures they had in the cell.

Dr. Small cleared his throat. It was only then that the kids remembered to thank him. The two older girls went to him.

Sonya said, "Thanks for rescuing us."

Dr. Small smiled at the girls.

"You are very lucky," he said. "A few more minutes and you'd be stuck in there forever."

Lynelle smiled at Dr. Small, "I'm sorry I doubted you and your machine."

Dr. Small opened a drawer and removed two small packages.

"Now kids," he said, "this machine is top secret. We can't talk about it to anyone."

"Not even my teacher?" Giselle asked.

"Not even your teacher."

"They won't believe us anyway," Justin answered glumly, remembering Mrs. Jones' and Ms. Simon's reactions.

Dr. Small handed the packages to Lynelle and Sonya, who immediately opened them. In them were two watches with plastic bands. The face of each watch was square with a two-inch touch screen.

"These," he said, "Will tell you everything you need to know about cells and just about everything else."

"Wow!" Lynelle exclaimed excitedly. "Thank you so much!"

Sonya was pensive.

"We can't accept such expensive gifts," she said. "We tampered with your machine and we messed up your experiment."

Dr. Small stood. He towered over the children.

"You kids have just proved to me that my invention works. Not only can it shrink people, but it can make them big again. Thanks to you, my experiment is a success."

Sonya touched the screen of her watch and it projected on to the wall.

"That watch is so cool!" Justin exclaimed. "Can I have one, too?"

"Me too," Giselle said.

Dr. Small shook his head and gave Justin and Giselle a book each.

"Those watches are very special. They come with great responsibility. I'm afraid you two kids aren't old enough to be entrusted with it."

Justin frowned, but accepted the book.

Dr. Small looked at Lynelle and Sonya.

"Whatever you do, don't let these watches out of your sight," he said.

Dr. Small ushered the kids out of the room. He led them to the cafeteria, where the other children had already gathered.

"Where have you been?" Mrs Jones said to Justin. "We were looking all over for you." She noticed the girls. "And what in the world happened to you three? You're soaking wet!"

Lynelle, Giselle, Sonya and Justin looked at each other. They didn't know what to say. Dr. Small answered for them, "They wanted to learn more about the cell, so I gave them a detailed lesson, including a 3D simulation. Getting wet is part of the simulation."

"Well, I expect a full report from both of you," Mrs. Jones said to the fifth grade girls. To Dr. Small she said, "Thank you for taking care of them."

The kids looked at Dr. Small and smiled their gratitude. He winked at them and was off.

"So what do we do now?" asked Giselle.

"Let's get some lunch, I'm hungry," Lynelle replied.

"I have to go to the bathroom," Sonya said.

A few minutes later the girls heard Sonya give an ear-piercing scream.

Lynelle laughed and looked at Giselle, "I think she just saw her hair."

CPSIA information can be obtained at www.ICGtesting.com
Printed in the USA
BVOW03s1304260814

364232BV00001B/1/P